A GARDEN FOR MISS MOUSE

To librarians, parents, and teachers:

A Garden for Miss Mouse is a Parents Magazine READ ALOUD Original — one title in a series of colorfully illustrated and fun-to-read stories that young readers will be sure to come back to time and time again.

Now, in this special school and library edition of *A Garden for Miss Mouse,* adults have an even greater opportunity to increase children's responsiveness to reading and learning — and to have fun every step of the way.

When you finish this story, check the special section at the back of the book. There you will find games, projects, things to talk about, and other educational activities designed to make reading enjoyable by giving children and adults a chance to play together, work together, and talk over the story they have just read.

For a free color catalog describing Gareth Stevens' list of high-quality books, call 1-800-341-3569 (USA) or 1-800-461-9120 (Canada).

Parents Magazine READ ALOUD Originals:

Golly Gump Swallowed a Fly
The Housekeeper's Dog
Who Put the Pepper in the Pot?
Those Terrible Toy-Breakers
The Ghost in Dobbs Diner
The Biggest Shadow in the Zoo
The Old Man and the Afternoon Cat
Septimus Bean and His Amazing Machine
Sherlock Chick's First Case
A Garden for Miss Mouse
Witches Four
Bread and Honey

Pigs in the House
Milk and Cookies
But No Elephants
No Carrots for Harry!
Snow Lion
Henry's Awful Mistake
The Fox with Cold Feet
Get Well, Clown-Arounds!
Pets I Wouldn't Pick
Sherlock Chick and the Giant
  Egg Mystery

Library of Congress Cataloging-in-Publication Data

Muntean, Michaela.
    A garden for Miss Mouse / by Michaela Muntean ; pictures by Christopher Santoro. — North American library ed.
        p. cm. — (Parents magazine read aloud original)
    Summary: Miss Mouse plants a garden which soon becomes more than she can handle.
    ISBN 0-8368-0891-6
    [1. Mice—Fiction. 2. Gardening—Fiction. 3. Stories in rhyme.] I. Title. II. Series.
    PZ8.3.M89Gar 1993
    [E]—dc20   92-27114

This North American library edition published in 1992 by Gareth Stevens Publishing, 1555 North RiverCenter Drive, Suite 201, Milwaukee, Wisconsin 53212, USA, under an arrangement with Parents Magazine Press, New York.

Text © 1982 by Michaela Muntean. Illustrations © 1982 by Christopher Santoro. Portions of end matter adapted from material first published in the newsletter *From Parents to Parents* by the Parents Magazine Read Aloud Book Club, © 1988 by Gruner + Jahr, USA, Publishing; other portions © 1992 by Gareth Stevens, Inc.

Printed in the United States of America

1 2 3 4 5 6 7 8 9 98 97 96 95 94 93

A GARDEN
FOR
MISS MOUSE

To R.H.S. for his
P.A.T.I.E.N.C.E.——*M.M.*

To Louise——*C.S.*

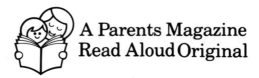 A Parents Magazine
Read Aloud Original

A GARDEN
FOR
MISS MOUSE

by

Michaela Muntean

pictures by

Christopher Santoro

Gareth Stevens Publishing
Milwaukee
Parents Magazine Press
New York

Every first of April
Miss Mouse tills and rakes and hoes.
Then she plants a garden
in neat and tidy rows.

A little row of carrots,
a little row of beans,
and then another little row
of lovely lettuce greens.

But this year when she started
to plant her little rows,
she stopped and said quite suddenly,
"This bores me to my toes!"

"I know what I will do!" she cried,
and then she danced a jig.
She grabbed her biggest shovel,
and she began to dig.

"I'll plant the biggest garden
ever seen by any mouse!"
Then up came every bit of land
all around her house.

Next she had to plant the seeds.
It took her all day long.
But all the while she planted,
she sang a planting song:

Plant a little of this,
and a little of that.
Cover the seed,
and give it a pat!

Every day she hoed and raked.
She tilled and pulled the weeds.

And soon green plants were springing up where she had planted seeds.

The plants all started growing.
They grew and grew and grew.
And everyone in Mouseville
came to *aah* and *ooh*.

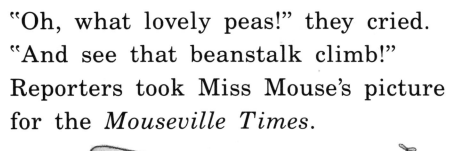

"Oh, what lovely peas!" they cried.
"And see that beanstalk climb!"
Reporters took Miss Mouse's picture
for the *Mouseville Times*.

EXTRA

The Mouseville Times

5¢

SEE HER GARDEN GROW!!

DATELINE MOUSEVILLE,

THE GARDEN OF MISS MOUSE HAS GROWN ENORMOUS! WHEN ASKED WHY SHE DID IT, MISS MOUSE CONFESSED, "THE SMALLER GARDEN SIMPLY BORED ME."

MISS MOUSE HAS GROWN LETTUCE, CARROTS, CELERY, AND BROCCOLI, TO NAME JUST A FEW OF HER VEGETABLES.

FOR A COMPLETE LISTING, TURN TO TODAY'S GARDENING SECTION.

NEIGHBORS REPORT THAT THEY ARE QUICKLY LOSING SIGHT OF THE HOUSE. THEY ARE STANDING BY IN CASE MISS MOUSE NEEDS THEIR HELP.

PHOTO: J. P. SQUEEK

SEE OUR EXCLUSIVE STORY ON MISS MOUSE INSIDE...

The garden grew much bigger,
and then it grew some more.
It covered all the windows,
it covered the front door!

That garden was enormous,
and the plants so very high,
that Miss Mouse used a flagpole
to get her laundry dry.

The mailman left her letters
atop a beanstalk vine,
while Miss Mouse proudly laughed and said,
"Isn't my garden fine!"

Then one day she woke to find
five mushrooms on her sheet,
ten pea pods on her pillow,
six peppers at her feet!

There were green beans in the basement,
and wax beans on the wall.

There was celery on the ceiling.
There were pumpkins in the hall!

Tomatoes in the bathtub!
Spinach on a chair!
Turnips on the table,
and zucchini *everywhere!*

Cabbage in the kitchen,
corn cobs in the hutch.
"Oh, my goodness!" cried Miss Mouse.
"My garden's grown too much!"

29

She knew she had to call for help,
but couldn't find the phone.
Then finally she found it
where some brussel sprouts had grown.

She called her best friend Field Mouse.
She asked him to come quick.
"Bring everyone you know!" she cried.
"There are vegetables to pick!"

So everyone in Mouseville
rushed out to help Miss Mouse.
"Where are you?" they cried helplessly.
"We cannot see your house!"

"My garden's growing everywhere!"
her friends could hear her shout.
"Please start picking vegetables
for I cannot get out!"

And so they started picking
fruit and vegetables galore.
They picked more kinds of vegetables
than you've seen in any store.

When finally they found Miss Mouse,
she cried, "How could I know
that this is what would happen
when things began to grow!"

"Don't worry," Field Mouse told her.
"It isn't all that bad.
We'll make the biggest salad
that we have ever had!"

All day they made that salad.
They chopped and tossed and peeled.

Then they had a garden party on Mouseville's football field.

BLUE CHEESE

"Good-bye and thank you," said Miss Mouse
when all her friends were going.
"Next year I'll keep my garden small.
It won't do too much growing!"

Notes to Grown-ups

Major Themes
Here is a quick guide to the significant themes and concepts at work in *A Garden for Miss Mouse:*

- The need to plan ahead (Miss Mouse didn't plan her garden, with almost disastrous results)
- Friendship, as shown by all the neighbors who helped to harvest Miss Mouse's crop

Step-by-step Ideas for Reading and Talking
Here are some ideas for further give-and-take between grown-ups and children. The following topics encourage creative discussion of *A Garden for Miss Mouse* and invite the kind of open-ended response that is consistent with many contemporary approaches to reading, including Whole Language:

- Encourage your child to create a story about following an idea to its extreme. Ask your child to make up a silly consequence of allowing a garden to grow unattended. A variation on this theme: make up a story about allowing a messy room to get out of hand. Or try anything at home that can get out of control, such as newspapers, magazines, toys, leaves in fall, ants on a flower stem, even cats in the street.
- The steps Miss Mouse took to plant and care for her garden are the ones used in any garden, or even, on a tiny scale, in a plant pot. This could be a good book to accompany a planting activity. For fast growth indoors year round, try mustard, cress, or alfalfa, all of which may be eaten in salads when they're only seedlings.
- Have your child identify the pictured vegetables by name and count the five mushrooms, ten pea pods, and six peppers on the bed.

Games for Learning

Children love to peel, stir, shake, mash, and bake. In short, like Miss Mouse and her friends, they like to prepare and cook things to eat. In additon to learning how ingredients mix together, cooking activities give children's fine motor muscles (the muscles they use in writing) exercise and training. (A child who can stir in a circle can make a letter O more easily.) Here are some suggestions for cooking activities that you and your child can do together:

Granola Cookies

You will need the following:

> 2 cups (500 ml) honey almond granola
> 2/3 cup (167 ml) sweetened condensed milk
> 1 teaspoon (5 ml) almond extract
> 1/4 teaspoon (1.25 ml) ginger
> red candied cherries

Preheat oven to 325°F (163°C).

While you hold the bowl, let your child stir the first four ingredients until well-blended. Drop the mixture by teaspoonsful onto foil-lined cookie sheets. Let your child cut the red candied cherries into quarters with a plastic serated knife. Garnish each cookie with a cherry piece. Bake fifteen minutes or until firm. Cool on the cookie sheets and peel the foil from the cookies.

Butter

Shaking cream into butter is a fun way to direct your child's pent-up energy on a rainy day. Just put whipping cream into a small glass jar with a tight-fitting lid, and take turns shaking it until you see the cream begin to thicken. Then keep shaking until it separates into butter and buttermilk. Pour off the milk and shake some more until all the buttermilk is shaken out. Drain a final time, salt lightly, spread on a cracker, and enjoy!

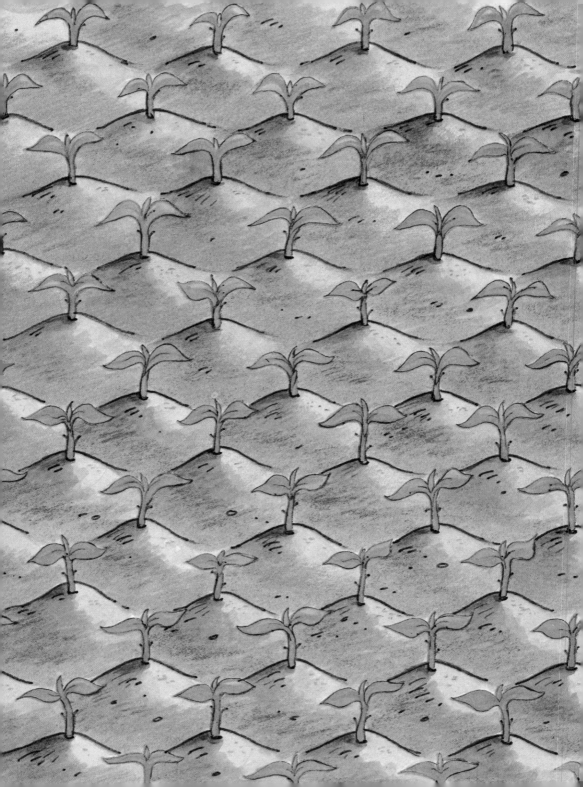

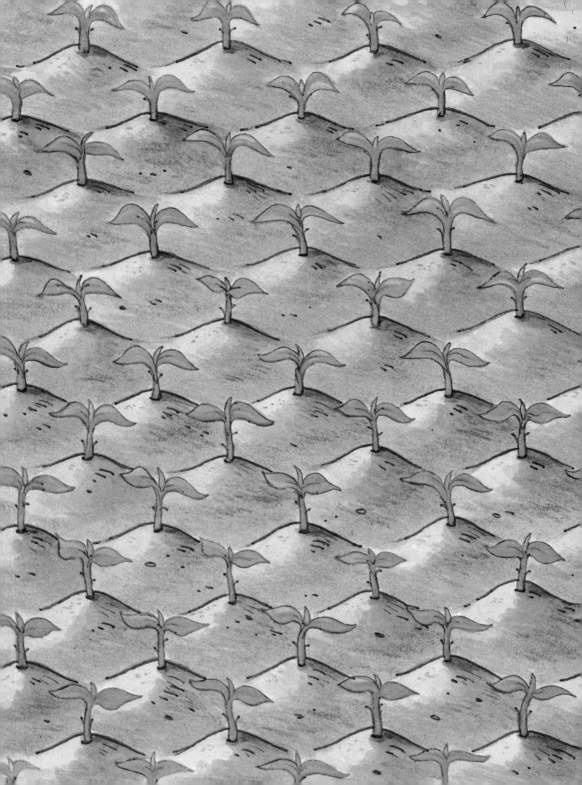

About the Author

MICHAELA MUNTEAN tried organic gardening one summer and, to her surprise, the tomato plants grew seven feet high! That's when *A Garden for Miss Mouse* was born.

Ms. Muntean was a children's book and magazine editor before she turned to writing full time. She has since written many well-loved children's books.

About the Artist

CHRISTOPHER SANTORO has a garden on the terrace of his apartment. But it's the apartment itself that reminds him of Miss Mouse's garden. "It's always overgrown with materials I use as models for the pictures I'm working on," he explains.

Mr. Santoro has illustrated many children's books, including another story written by Michaela Muntean.